Michael's class was learning about the Ten Commandments.

"When the Jewish people received the Torah," his teacher said, "they received the Ten Commandments, God's special rules that show us how to live. We should not hurt others, we should not steal, we should honor our parents," Miss Sharon explained.

"We also have special rules here at school," she continued. "Can you think of some rules we have in our classroom?"

"You shouldn't hit anyone," Julie answered.

"Or stand on the furniture," added Sam.

"You should share toys," said David.

"And help at cleanup time," Rachel noted.

Michael was sitting with a frown on his face. Miss Sharon looked at him and asked, "Do you have something to add, Michael?"

"I don't like rules," Michael replied. "It would be a lot more fun if we could do whatever we wanted. School would be the best place if we didn't have any rules."

Miss Sharon smiled and said, "All right, Michael. Tomorrow we won't have any rules in our classroom. Then you can decide if you like having rules."

"YIPPEE!" shouted Michael.

The next morning Michael ran into the classroom, excited that there would be no rules. Suddenly he tripped over Julie's backpack and nearly fell to the floor.

"Hey, Julie, your backpack is supposed to be in your cubby!" yelled Michael.

"No it's not!" replied Julie. "THERE ARE NO RULES TODAY."

Michael shrugged and walked over to the puzzle table. As he began working on a puzzle, Rachel grabbed one of the pieces.

"I need that piece!" cried Michael. "Give it back!"

"THERE AREN'T ANY RULES TODAY," Rachel reminded him with a giggle. "I don't have to share."

At circle time, Michael wanted to show his friends his new dinosaur, but no one would listen to him. David was racing his new car back and forth across the floor as several of the children squealed with delight.

"You have to be quiet. It's my turn now!" Michael demanded.

"No we don't," responded David. "THERE ARE NO RULES TODAY."

On the playground, Michael waited for his turn on the tricycle. Sam was pretending to be a firefighter racing to a burning building. He zoomed by Michael several times. *"Wooo,"* he screamed, trying to sound like a siren.

"May I have a turn now, Sam?" Michael asked hopefully.

"Nooo," sang Sam in his siren voice. "THERE ARE NOOO RULES TOOODAY."

At snack time, Jonah playfully grabbed some of Michael's crackers without asking. Michael didn't say anything. THERE ARE NO RULES TODAY, he thought sadly, as a tear slid down his cheek.

"What's wrong, Michael?" Miss Sharon asked gently.

"I thought having no rules would be fun," Michael tearfully replied. "I could do whatever I wanted. But I haven't been able to do anything I want today. No one will listen to me. No one will give me a turn. No one will share.

"I guess rules are important. Rules show people how to care about each other."

Miss Sharon hugged Michael. "You're right," she agreed. "That's why God gave us the Ten Commandments. And that's why we have rules here at school. We need to treat others the way we want to be treated."

"Do you think we could have our rules back tomorrow?" asked Michael.

"How about right now?" replied Miss Sharon with a smile. "Children, when you finish your snack, it's cleanup time."

"YIPPEE!" shouted Michael, as he rushed to be the first one to pick up the toys.

The 10 Commandments:
A Child-Friendly Version

1. There is only one God.
2. God is so amazing that no one can draw a picture or make anything that looks like God.
3. God's name is very special and should be said with great care.
4. Shabbat is the most special day of the week – a day to rest and enjoy the world around us.
5. Honor and listen to your parents.
6. Life is precious. Do not hit or hurt anyone.
7. Married people should respect each other.
8. Do not take anything that doesn't belong to you.
9. Always tell the truth. Do not tell lies.
10. Be happy with what you have. Don't be jealous of other people or what they have.

The Ten Commandments:
Exodus, Chapter 20

1. I am the Lord your God.
2. You shall have no other gods besides Me. You shall not make for yourself a sculptured image, or any likeness of what is in the heavens above, or on the earth below, or in the waters under the earth. You shall not bow down to them or serve them.
3. You shall not swear falsely by the name of the Lord your God.
4. Remember the Sabbath day and keep it holy.
5. Honor your father and your mother.
6. You shall not murder.
7. You shall not commit adultery.
8. You shall not steal.
9. You shall not bear false witness.
10. You shall not covet . . . anything that is your neighbor's.